Two Festivals

by

Eliza Lee Cabot Follen

Double9 BOOKS

Two Festivals
by Eliza Lee Cabot Follen

ISBN: 978-93-74832-36-3

Published by

DOUBLE 9 BOOKS
2/13-B, Ansari Road
Daryaganj, New Delhi – 110002
info@double9books.com
www.double9books.com
Tel. 011-40042856

ABOUT THE AUTHOR

Eliza Lee Cabot Follen was an influential American writer, editor, and abolitionist born on August 15, 1787, in Boston, Massachusetts. She was known for her contributions to various papers and magazines, writing both prose and poetry. A dedicated abolitionist, she worked tirelessly to promote the cause of ending slavery in the United States. In 1828, she married Professor Charles Follen, a German immigrant and fellow abolitionist, who tragically died aboard the Lexington in 1840. This loss deeply affected Follen, yet she continued to write and advocate for social justice throughout her life. Follen's works spanned genres, and she was especially known for her children's literature and moral essays. She was a passionate voice for women's rights and the abolition of slavery, often using her writing to inspire change and raise awareness. Follen passed away on January 26, 1860, in Brookline, Massachusetts, at the age of 72. She was the daughter of Samuel Cabot and Sarah Barrett, who provided her with a solid foundation in intellectual thought. Throughout her life, Eliza Lee Cabot Follen's work left an indelible mark on the fight for equality and justice in America.

CONTENTS

MAY MORNING AND NEW YEAR'S EVE

t is the evening before the first of May, and the boys are looking forward to a May-day festival with the children in the neighborhood. Mrs. Chilton read aloud these beautiful lines of Milton:—

Now the bright morning star, Day's harbinger,
Comes dancing from the east, and loads with her
The flowery May, who from her green lap throws
The yellow cowslip, and the pale primrose.
Hail beauteous May that dost inspire
Mirth, and youth, and warm desire;
Woods and groves arc of thy dressing,
Hill and dale doth boast thy blessing.
Thus we salute thee with our early song,
And welcome thee, and with thee long.

"How beautiful!" said Frank and Harry. "Suppose, Mother," said Harry, "it should rain, and hail, and snow to-morrow, for it looks like it now, and then you know we cannot go into the woods and gather flowers; and all our plans will be spoiled." "Why, then, my dear, we must enjoy May morning as the great poet did, after he lost his sight, with our mind's eye; and you must bear your disappointment patiently." "Easier said than done, Mother," said Harry. "Why, only think of all our preparations, and the beautiful wreath you made for Lizzy Evans, who is to be queen of the May, and how pretty she would look in it, and then think of the dinner in the woods, we all sitting round in a circle, and she and the king of the May in the midst of us, and Ned Brown playing on his flageolet; and then you know we are all to walk home in procession, and have a dance at his mother's after tea." "You will not lose your dance, Harry," said his mother, "if it should hail, and rain, and snow; but, on the contrary, enjoy it all the more, for then you will riot be fatigued by a long walk; and Lizzy can wear the wreath at any rate." "I don't care for the fatigue, Mother; I want to be in the woods and gather the flowers with my own hands, and smell them as I gather them in the fresh air, and hear the birds sing; and to scream as loud as I please, and kick up my heels, and not hear any one say, 'Don't make such a noise, Harry.' I guess Milton did not take as much pleasure in writing poetry about the spring after he became blind. But please read his May Song again, Mother." She read it again.

"I think he must have felt as glad when he wrote it," said Harry, "as I hope to feel tomorrow.—'Comes dancing from the east'—how beautiful it is! What a pity he ever lost his sight!" "Milton," said the mother, "made such a good use of his eyes while he could see, that he laid up stores of beautiful images, which he remembered when he could no longer use his bodily eyes. The poetry he wrote when he was blind shows the most accurate observation of the outward appearances of things, of shades of color, and of all those beauties which only sight could have taught him. It is worth while, boys, for you to imitate him in this, while you admire his poetry."

May morning came. It did not hail, or rain, or snow. The sun shone brightly. The birds seemed to know as well as the children that it was the first of May. The country village in which Mrs. Chilton lived was as noisy as a martin box, at break of day, when doubtless, though we poor wingless bipeds don't understand what the birds are chattering about, they are planning their work and their amusements for the day—and why not?

Soon after sunrise, all the children from far and near, dressed in their holiday clothes, with little baskets of provisions, all assembled on a little green before Mrs. Grey's house, and were ready to set out for the woods, about two miles distant. Ned Brown had his flageolet, and another boy had a drum. Lizzy Evans received the wreath which made her queen of the May, and Frank, being the tallest boy, was chosen king. And now off they all set, in high glee, happy as only children can be.

Mrs. Chilton, and the teacher of the village school had promised the children to join them at the dinner hour, which was twelve. Just about eleven, the clouds began to gather. Nevertheless, the ladies kept their promise, and set out for the wood. The threatened shower came up, and they took refuge in an old empty barn, where they had not been many minutes before all the children, one after the other, came dripping in, some laughing, some small ones crying. Soon, however, the laughers prevailed; and, after showing their flowers, of which they had collected many, they set themselves to work to spread out the dinner, in the most attractive way possible, and make what amends they could for the unlucky chance of the rain. An old milk stool was appropriated to the queen. It had not even the accustomed number of three legs to support it, so that the poor queen had to endure the anxiety of a tottering throne, and learned experimentally some of the pains of royalty. The king took possession of an old barrel that had lost both ends, and sitting astride upon it, Bacchus fashion he took his place by the side of the poor queen on her two-legged stool, upon which she was exercising all the art of balancing that she had acquired in one quarter at dancing school, hoping against hope that she might keep her dignity from rolling on the barn floor. Just as his May-majesty was fairly seated on the barrel, it, all at once, fell in, smash, and he was half covered with old hoops and slaves. Whereupon the queen laughed so immoderately as to lose her balance, and thus both rolled in the dust. In the mean time, the other children, who had no dignity to support, had spread their little repast on an old sledge. Mrs. Chilton, who had brought a table-cloth, assisted them. Dinner was now announced. The queen declared she could support her throne no longer, and she and the king, both forgetting their royalty, sat down with the others on the hay-strewn floor, and discussed apples, cake, &c., &c.

Unfortunately the rain lasted longer than the dinner; every scrap that was eatable of their provisions was consumed; and now the children all looked around with that peculiar, beseeching, half-discontented look, which is their wont to have on such occasions, as much as to say, "What shall we do next?" Grown people who have been much with children, know full well that there is no peace when such symptoms appear, under such circumstances, unless, before the king of misrule begins his reign, something is proposed of a composing tendency for turbulent spirits. Accordingly, Mrs. Chilton asked the children if they had ever heard of the Mayday ball which is given every year to the children in Washington. "No," was the answer. She said she had been at one, and she would tell all about it.

"It is held in a large public hall, decorated for the purpose. All the children in Washington and Georgetown are invited to attend; all have an equal right to go, ignorant and educated, poor and rich; no matter how poor, if the girls can get a neat white frock, and the boys a decent dress, they are all admitted; every one wears a wreath of flowers, or has a bouquet in his hand or bosom. The children assemble very early, and dance as much as they please, to the music of a fine band, and all partake of some simple refreshment, provided for them, before they return home. They number often over a thousand, and as they are all moving together to the music, they look like a dancing flower garden. I said all the children, rich and poor, in Washington. I wish it were so; but there are many poor children who are never invited to this festival. No one dresses one of them in a nice white frock on May morning, and puts a wreath of flowers on her head, and a nosegay in her hands, and says to her, 'Go, dance, sing, and rejoice with the other children in God's beautiful world.'"

"Why not?" asked the listening children.

"They are slaves—they are negroes!" replied Mrs. Chilton.

"It is a shame; it is wicked," cried Frank and Harry, and all the rest.

"When you are men and women," said Mrs. Chilton, "you may do much for the poor slaves. Remember them then, and do not forget them now. All can do something for them, even little children.

Now I will tell you a story that was related to me by a gentlemen who knew it to be true. I knew, he said, a little boy, who was one of the best little fellows that ever lived. He was gentle and kind to his companions, obedient to his parents, good to all. His home was in a small country village, but he was very fond of wandering into the neighboring fields, when his tasks were all over. There, if he saw a young bird that had fallen to the ground before it could fly, he would pick it up gently, and put it back in its nest. I have often seen him step aside, lest he should tread on an anthill, and thus destroy the industrious little creatures' habitation. If a child smaller than he was carrying a heavy bundle or basket, Harry would always offer to help him. Was any one hurt, or unhappy, Harry was quick to give aid and sympathy; ever ready to defend the weak, feared not the strong. For every harsh word, Harry gave a kind one in return. I have known him to carry more than half his breakfast to a little lame boy whose mother was very poor. Harry was brave and true; he would confess his own faults, he would hide those of others. He had a thirst for knowledge. He got all his lessons well at school, and he stood high in his class. But what he was particularly remarkable for, was his love of all beautiful things, and most especially of wild flowers. He would make wreaths of them and give them to his mother, and he was very fond of putting one on my study table, when he could contrive to place it there without my seeing him. Harry knew all the green nooks where the houstonia was to be found in the early spring, and it was he that ever brought me the beautiful gentian that opens its fringed petals in the middle of the chilly October day. On Sunday, and on all holidays, Harry always had a flower or a bit of green in the button-hole of his jacket. Every sunny window in his mother's house had an old teapot or broken pitcher in it, containing one of Harry's plants whose bright blossoms hid defects and infirmities. He also loved music passionately; he whistled so sweetly that it was a delight to hear him. Yet there was something in his notes that always went to your heart and made you sad, they were so mournful.

Often in the summer time, he would go, towards evening, into the fields and lie down in the long grass; and there he would look straight up into the clear deep blue sky, and whistle such plaintive tunes, that, beautiful as they were, it made your heart ache to hear them. You could not see him, and it seemed as if you were listening to the song of a spirit.

Alas! Harry was not happy; God's glorious world was all around him; his soul was tuned to the harmony of heaven, and yet his young heart ached; and tears—bitter, scalding tears—often ran down his smooth, round cheek, and then he would run and hide his head in his mother's lap, that blessed home for a troubled spirit.

One day, I discovered the cause of Harry's melancholy. I was returning from a walk, and saw him at a little brook that ran behind my house, washing his face and hands vehemently, and rubbing them very hard. I then remembered that I had often seen him there doing the same thing. "It seems to me, Harry," I said, "that your face and hands are clean now; why do you rub your face so violently?" "I am trying," he said, "to wash away this color. I can never be happy till I get rid of this color. If I wash me a great deal, will it not come off at last! The boys will not play with me; they do not love me because I am of this color; they are all white. Why, if God is good, did he not make me white?" And he wept bitterly. "Poor dear little boy!" I said, and took him in my arms and pressed him to my heart! "God is good; it is man that is cruel." The little fellow was soothed and strengthened by my sympathy, and the counsel I gave him.

Not long after this, it was May-day, and all the children of the village went out into the fields to gather flowers, to dress themselves for a little dance they were to have in the evening. Every boy and girl in the village, except Harry, was of the party. They set off early in the morning, and they ran gayly over hills and meadows, and hunted busily for flowers; but the spring had been cold, and they could not find many. They were returning home, wearied, and rather chilled and disheartened, when they saw Harry coming out of the woods with a large bunch of flowers in his hand. One of the boys called out to him, "Well, nigger, where did you get all your flowers?" Harry went on and made no answer. "Come, stop, darky," said the hard-hearted boy, "stop, and let's have your flowers; here's three cents for them." "I don't wish to sell them," said Harry; "they are all for my mother." "A nigger carry flowers to his mother! that's a good one! Come, boys, let's take them from him; they are as much our flowers as his; he has gathered more than his share;" and he approached Harry to seize his flowers.

"For shame, Tom, for shame!" cried out many of the children, and one of the larger boys came forward and stood by Harry. "Touch him if you dare, Tom. You have got to knock me down first." The cruel boy, who was, of course, a coward, fell back, and some of the little children gathered around Harry to look at the flowers. "Don't mind that naughty boy, Harry," said one little girl, and slid her little hand into his. Harry's anger was always conquered by one word of kindness. "Where did you get all your flowers?" asked the children. "I will show you," replied Harry, "if you will follow me." They all shouted, "Let's go, let's go; show us the way, Harry;" and off they set. Harry ran like a quail through bush and brier, and over rocks and stone walls, till he came to a hill covered with a wood. "On the other side of this hill," said he, "we shall find them." In a very few minutes the children were all there. There they saw a warm, sunny hollow; through it ran a little brook, and all around were massive rocks and pretty nooks; and there were the birds singing loudly, and there were cowslips, and anemones, and houstonias, and violets, and all in great profusion. The boy who had insulted Harry hung back ashamed. Harry quietly said to him, "Here, under this little tree, is a beautiful bed of violets, and there are anemones." Harry tasted of the pleasure of doing good for evil. The boy who had defended him walked by him, and talked kindly to him. "How good it was in you to show us the flowers!" said the little girl who had taken Harry's hand, and whose apron he had filled with flowers. How happy now was poor Harry!

All the children gathered that morning as many flowers as they desired. Some carried home only perishable earthly flowers in their hands; others, immortal flowers in their hearts. The village children went to their dance, and were very happy. Harry spent the rest of the day and the evening in his mother's cottage, alone with her, and amused himself with making wreaths of his flowers. But he said he had never passed so happy a May-day. A loving heart, like Una's beauty, 'can make a sunshine in a shady place.'"

The clouds had now passed away. One of the boys proposed to pass a vote of thanks to the old barn, for the hospitable shelter it had afforded during the shower. This was received and passed with acclamations. Frank and Lizzy, or rather the king and queen of the May, declared that they had no thanks to offer to the old barrel or the milk stool. It was too wet to go into the woods again; so they formed a procession, and with their flowers in their hands, and such music as they had, returned gayly home.

The children all enjoyed the dance in the evening; but there were some hearts there, young and merry as they were, that made a solemn vow never to forget those of whom they had heard that day,—"them that are in bonds."

It is New Year's eve. Frank and Harry are sitting with their mother by the pleasant fireside. The boys were full of chat, but their mother was looking fixedly into the fire, and had been silent for a long time. She was thinking of the past; they, of what was to come.

"Mother," said Harry, "will you tell me tonight what my new year's gift will be?"

"Don't speak to mother now," said Frank.

"Why not?

"O, because mother looks as if she did not want to talk."

"But mother told me that, if I would be silent till she had done reading, I might talk as much as I pleased to her."

"So I did, Harry," said his mother; "and now I am ready to hear you. What did you ask me?"

"Only, Mother, whether you meant I should know what my new year's gift is, before tomorrow morning."

"No, dear; I think you had better have it all new and fresh to-morrow; the surprise is a part of the pleasure of a new year's gift."

"What can it be? I know what I hope it is."

"What do you hope it will be, Harry?"

"I do hope it will be a magic lantern," said Harry, without a moment's hesitation. His mother made no answer.

"What do you wish for?" asked Harry.

"I don't know," said Frank; "there are so many things I wish for, that I hardly know what to say first."

"I wish," said their mother, "that I could grant all your wishes; that I could give you every good thing you desire; but my means, as you know, are limited. I am sorry, dear, that you have so many wishes ungratified."

"O Mother, it is not for such things as you can give that I most wish for. You are very kind to me, and give me more good things than you ought to give me; you are too generous to me. I wish for what no one can give me."

"We all have many such wishes, my dear child; but we must not think even these quite unattainable. There are few things that a reasonable being earnestly desires, that some day or other may not become his."

"Do you think so, Mother?"

"Yes, Frank; perhaps he may not attain them in this life, but I think the very desire is a prophecy, and even promise, that we shall at some stage of our being possess what we wish."

"I know what I shall wish, then," said Harry, "and keep wishing it as long as I live till I get it, though I am afraid I shall never have it. I'll tell you what my wish is, Frank, if you will tell me yours."

"Agreed, Harry," said Frank; "and you shall tell your wish first, and I last."

"I wish," said Harry, "that I had a flying horse that was perfectly gentle, and would go all over the world with me, and do just as I told him to, and never be tired; but I guess I never shall get one. Come, Frank, what do you wish?"

"I wish that I had a great deal of strength and courage, more than any one else, and was never afraid of any thing, and that I could do whatever was to be done, and become, at last, a great man, and do some good in the world. I don't want to sit still in a corner half of my life, and never use my faculties. Now, Mother, Harry and I have told our wishes; will you tell yours?"

"First," said the mother, "let me show you how near you may, even in this life, come to your wishes, and then I will tell mine. Harry will not continue to wish for a flying horse, because he will know he can never have it in this world; but his wish will change into a desire of travelling and seeing all that is beautiful and wonderful in God's glorious world, and then he will find his flying horse in a rail carriage or steamboat. And you, my dear Frank, if you continue to wish to be strong and brave, and truly great, will have, perhaps, more than you ask for; for, if you do not have a strong body, you will have a brave spirit, and you will be what is better than a strong man—a good, great man. True greatness does not depend upon physical strength; for instance, a brave and noble woman may be greater than a man."

"How is that, Mother?"

"Because, from the weakness of her body she has more obstacles to overcome. Her power arises from an inward strength that lasts long, and shines most brightly in the darkest hour of trial. Mere bodily strength, without this power of soul, is often cowardly and useless.

I will tell you a true story that I heard the other day, which will show you what I mean. Somewhere in the State of Maine there is a beautiful little lake, on the banks of which are a number of farms and pleasant dwelling houses. There are boats on the lake, and the people are in the habit of allowing the children to learn early the management of a boat; girls and boys together are allowed to go out on the lake, without any man to take charge of them. One day, a little party went out. They had been rowing about for some time, and gathering pond lilies, and waking up all the echoes in the surrounding woods with loud shouts, merry laughs, and happy songs. The children were in the middle of the lake, and were thinking of returning, when, by some accident, one of the boys fell overboard. A boy of fourteen years of age had the management of the boat; he was the principal oarsman. He was strong and active, and could swim, but he feared for his own life, and he immediately began to row for the shore to get help. In the mean time, the poor boy, who could not swim to the shore, and whose strength would be unequal to keep above water till they returned with help, would have been drowned. There were other boys in the boat, but it was a little girl, of ten years of age, who, immediately forgetting her weakness, became their leader and guide. She insisted that the boat should be turned back again, that the poor boy should not be left. I know not if she seized the oar, but if she did not, she prevailed with others to turn the boat round and come back again to the poor boy, who, seeing himself left by his companions, was giving himself up for lost. As soon as they came up to him again, the brave

little girl asked the boy of fourteen years to keep the boat as steady as he could. Then she reached over the side of the boat, and told her companions to hold her fast by the legs. Soon she was able to reach the drowning boy. He was much bigger than she. She told him to put his arms round her neck. She then put her arms under his, and pulled him safely into the boat.

This girl was a small, delicate child. Now, dear Frank, who was the strong and brave one, the girl or the boy? Which would you rather be?"

"Of course, the girl, Mother. What a brave little soul she was!"

"So you see, Frank, that what is most truly desirable in your wish is within your reach, even now."

"She was a first rate girl," said Harry, "and the boy was a real coward for going away and leaving the poor fellow in the lake;" and he breathed a long breath, as if he had himself just come out of the water.

"Now, boys, to match that story of the little girl, I will tell you one of a sailor boy who was even braver and nobler than she. As a schooner was sailing near Montauk Point, Long Island, she was suddenly struck by a heavy gust of wind, upset, and instantly sunk. A vessel near by, which had seen the calamity, sent its boat to save from sinking any that had not gone to the bottom. On coming near where the schooner went down, they saw a little boy, twelve years old, floating on some wood, and went to take him off. As they approached him, he cried out, 'Never mind me; save the captain; he has a wife and six children. Both, however, were saved. Can we make any better resolution, my dear boys," said Mrs. Chilton, "to begin the New Year with, than that we will try to be as brave and self-forgetting as the little girl and boy I have been telling you about? And now, good night."

"Good night, old year, for the last time," said Harry; and they were soon asleep.

On New Year's morning, Harry found a large bag hanging to his bed post, containing a magic lantern; and Frank saw on his bureau a complete set of Miss Edgeworth's Works.

Again it is New Year's eve. Another year has passed happily over the home of Mrs. Chilton and her boys.

"To-morrow, dear Mother, is New Year's day," said Frank; "may we not, as we are one year older, sit up till the clock strikes twelve, and wish you a happy new year before we go to bed?"

"Yes, boys, if you can keep awake, you may sit up. Tell me, Frank, do you think you have gained as much this year as you ought to have gained? Ere long you will be a man."

"I think I have gained something," replied Frank. "I am at the head of my class in school. I am three inches taller, I am stronger, and I know a great deal more than I did last year."

"Is that all you have gained? Have you cured any of your faults? Can you command your temper any better? Are you any more disinterested? Are you more careful about the truth—in short, are you a better boy?"

"I cannot say, Mother; you know about that better than I."

"You expect a New Year's gift to-morrow, I presume, Frank."

"Yes, Mother, you always give us a New Year's gift, you know. Will you let us sit up till the clock strikes twelve to-night?"

Their mother promised that they should, and added, "I have been thinking of a New Year's gift for you, Frank, that I am not quite sure you will like. I will tell you what it is, and if you do not like it, you will say so honestly, I trust."

"What is it, Mother?"

"You know the little room I call my closet. It has a window in it, and contains some shelves with books on them. I propose to give you that closet, with all the books I shall leave in it, for your own. In it are a desk and a chair. From the window, you look directly, you know, upon the pine grove. In this little room, you may study and write and read and think also, as much as you please."

Frank could scarcely hear his mother finish, for delight at the thought. "All my own? the books, the desk, the nice old-fashioned chair and the closet itself? Why, Mother, I never should have believed you would have given it to me for my own. There is nothing I should like so well in the world. Shall I have the Shakespeare, and the Johnson, and the Classical Dictionary, and the Sir Charles Grandison, and all the old poets, and those French books in it, and the Homer and the Virgil too?"

"Yes, my son, I think I need not ask you to promise to lend them to me when I wish to borrow them. I have a great affection for this closet, Frank, and therefore I give it to you. If the walls could speak, they could tell you a great deal of your mother's history."

"I wish they could; I shall sit there a great deal, and I should like to hear all they have to say."

"As I have promised you to let you sit up till the new year comes in, I will tell you something now of what they would say. You know that this is the house in which I was born, so that this closet knew me from a child. Many a time, when I was a little girl, has my mother shut me up in it for refusing to obey her. It was gentle treatment shutting me up in this closet;

had it not been called a punishment, I never should have thought it one. In summer time, the whispering of the wind through the pine trees rebuked my bad temper, and seemed to say, 'Hush, Alice! Peace! Be still.' I always came out better than I went into it. When I was nine years old, my father gave me this closet for my own use altogether. Many of the books that are in it now were in it then, and the same desk and chair stand there to this day. My father had just built on to his house the addition which gave him the library which I now use; his law books and papers, &c., required better accommodation; and, from that time, the closet became mine. He gave it to me, as I do to you, for a New Year's gift; and this is one reason why I love to give it to you for the same purpose. It is a very dear and sacred spot to me, Frank, this closet, and I think you will like to hear something of its history."

"Yes, indeed I shall, Mother," said Frank.

"When I first took possession of it," continued his mother, "I felt more grand, I fancy, than Queen Victoria did when she took possession of the throne of England, for she had anticipated her elevation, whereas I had never dreamed of mine. When I was a girl, children did not fare as they do now, and my father's liberality to me was an unusual thing. My father and mother both went up stairs with me on New Year's day, and led me into my little sanctum, which they had dressed with evergreens, and seated me in the three-cornered leather-bottomed chair, and told me that every thing in the closet was mine. Although it was winter, still the pine trees that you know come so near the window, and that now are old trees, looked beautiful, and to me it seemed a little paradise. 'Here,' said my mother, 'you were many a time shut up by me in order to make you a good girl. Now you are old enough to know yourself when it is the right time for you to be shut up here, in order that you may grow good. I advise you, at such times, to come here and stay till you have conquered the bad spirit, and can come out with a firm resolution to do better. I shall never put you in the closet again, but I shall trust, Alice, that you will put yourself in, at all proper times.' I well remember putting my arms around my mother's neck and kissing her for joy, but I said not a word. My heart was too full of love, and gratitude, and pleasure to speak. After my parents left me in the closet, in my own chair, now all my own, I sat still some minutes thinking what I should do with my great possession, how I should improve my great blessing. The thought of my mother's loving trust in me affected me very much. I resolved I would not disappoint her. I resolved that, whenever I found myself doing wrong, I would come to my closet, shut myself in, and pray there for strength to cure my faults. I then counted them all over as far as I knew them, and resolved to get rid of them all. I was too happy to think of the difficulty in the way of doing this, but my self-confidence was soon rebuked. After looking over all the books, and putting my fingers upon every thing in my little kingdom, and dancing up and down with delight, I followed my father and mother down stairs to see the presents for the other children. Such was my state of exaltation that when my little sister came, full of joy, to me, with her new doll, I turned contemptuously away from her, and sneered at it, and said, 'Who wants to look at a doll? My New Year's gift is the best; it is worth yours and the boys' all put together.' Never shall I forget the grieved, disappointed look of my little sister as she said, 'Why, Alice, I thought you would be so glad to see my doll,'—and never shall I forget the silent rebuke of my mother's gentle eye, as she looked at me sadly. I felt it all. I could not stand it. I ran up to my closet; I turned the key as I closed the door. I fell on my knees and poured forth to my Father in heaven the first TRUE prayer I ever remember to have uttered. I prayed for forgiveness of my unkindness, I prayed for strength to conquer my many faults.

That day I did not sin again. I played with Fanny's doll. I did all that I could to make every one happy. I took the children up to my closet, and tried to make them share in all my pleasures while I tried to enjoy theirs. I made amends for my fault. From that time, I began a religious self-scrutiny and censorship. I watched myself very carefully, and for every fault I did penance in my closet. When I shut myself up on account of wrong doing, I would not allow myself to read or do any thing but think of my fault. The words of my mother which had been uttered without much serious thought, were as a law to me. I became, if possible, too sensitive to my own defects; it made me rather egotistical. It seemed as if my heart had become suddenly changed. I was, as it were, born again; a new life began in me.

One penance that I subjected myself to was to go and confess to my mother all my faults, even the most trifling. She feared that this continual self-reference would make me, as it did, an egotist, and she, one day, advised me to be satisfied with seeing my wrong doings and acknowledging them to myself, and to try to correct them without speaking of them to her. I begged her, with tears, to let me have my own way, for that telling her all helped me greatly; and I think, for a time, it did. The necessity of confiding all that is in our hearts, and all we do that is wrong, to a being whom we entirely respect and love, and in whose purity we confide, is a great check upon evil thoughts and evil deeds. One instance I well remember of the good effect of my confession. My mother insisted upon careful and neat habits in all things. She would not allow us to throw down our caps or bonnets. They must all be hung up on pegs in the hall, and each child had a peg of his or her own. As we often forgot the command, our mother, in order to remind us, made a law, one winter, that whoever broke the rule should, when the apples were distributed in the evening, have none. One day, all of us came in to supper in haste from play, and two out of four of us forgot to hang up their hats—my sister was one, and I the other. The footman picked up my hat, and hung it up in the right place. At the time of distributing the apples, my mother gave me a fine one, and said, "Alice never forgets her hat. No one forgets now but Jeannie. She is very careless, and must have no apple to-night." I was mean enough to take my apple and be silent; but I could not eat it. Still there seemed to be a spell over me; and, wretched as I was, I could not speak and confess before my brothers and sisters how false and shabby I had been. I went to my closet; and there, after a while, I resolved that, in the morning, I would tell the whole truth. I went to bed, but I could not go to sleep. As soon as I heard my mother coming to bed, I went to her bedside, confessed the truth to her, gave her my apple, and begged her to tell the children how mean I had been. My mother was as just as she was kind. "You must tell them yourself," she said. "You must confess your fault to your youngest sister with your own lips, and be willing to appear before her what you are. You must not ask me to save you this disgrace. It is that which will cure you. It is your just punishment." I did as she bade me, and this was my last sin of that kind.

I had another fault, and that was a great irritability of temper, and many and many an hour of solitude have I passed in that closet, looking out at the quiet pine trees, and listening to the soft sighing of the winds through their branches, till my heart has been softened, and the spirit of love and gentleness has returned. I remember one instance in particular of my conquest there of my foolish anger. I was in the habit, in warm weather, of learning all my lessons in my closet, particularly favorite pieces of poetry, which I wished to commit well to memory. There I recited them aloud. I found that the other children would often come and listen to me; this fretted me; I was very angry at it. I desired them not to do it, and not in an amiable manner; but they often forgot or disregarded my request. I could not, or thought I could not, command my temper whenever I found this out. One day I had been reciting Hamlet's soliloquy; and, just after I had repeated the last words, I heard William say in a pompous manner, "Toby or not Toby." I was very angry, foolish as it may seem to you, and burst open the door so suddenly and violently that I threw down my little sister who stood against it; and, instead of taking her up, I told her I was glad I had knocked her down; and then I was coward enough to strike my little brother. The cries of both children brought up my mother. By this time, I had come to my senses. I told her the story just as it was, and I felt very much ashamed.

My mother simply said to me, "I thought you were beginning to be a reasonable being, and had ceased to be a passionate coward. You know that William is not so strong as you, or you would not dare to strike him." Her words seemed to me very harsh then, but now I think they were just. All abuse of power, all cruelty to the weak, is truly cowardly and mean.

That day I punished myself severely. Some friends were to dine with us, friends whom I loved particularly to see; one of them was Jane Grey, my earliest and dearest friend; but I would not go down to dinner. When called,

I sent a note to my mother, saying I should not come down, and wanted no dinner, and begging her not to send again for me, for it would be in vain. I heard the cheerful, merry voices of the family at dinner. I heard the birds singing in the trees near my window. I breathed in the sweet fragrance of the roses and the new hay. I saw the animals at a distance feeding quietly. The clear, deep-blue sky, as I gazed up at it from my window, looked so pure, so solemn, as if angels unseen might be hovering over the world. All, all but me was beautiful, and happy, and good. I was sinful, I was unhappy; I was, it seemed to me, a discord in the world. I hated myself for my bad temper, for it was some time before I had quite conquered it. At last, however, I did, and became gentle and happy in my chosen solitude, while others were enjoying themselves together.

In the middle of the afternoon, they all went out to walk. When Jeannie came up for her bonnet, she ran to my closet, and called out to me, "Dear Alice! mother told me not to come to you at dinner time; but we can't be happy without you. Jane says she can't play without you. Can't you come down? Do, Alice." "No," I replied. "Say nothing about me. I shall not see Jane to-day." After Jeannie left me, I could not quite keep the tears from my eyes. Pretty soon, my dear mother, who always thought people must suffer from hunger, came to me and brought me a nice piece of pudding she had saved for me, and said kindly to me, "Come, Alice, you have punished yourself enough; eat this pudding and come down stairs. You will not be so passionate again." I would not go down, but I ate the pudding. When our friends were all gone, I went down, and then I told Willie I was sorry for striking him. Whether it was that my partiality to Jane, which caused what I suffered that day to make a peculiarly deep impression on my mind, I know not; but, from that time, I acquired more self-command; and never did I forget that day in my closet.

I could tell you much more about my closet experiences, Frank, of what I have enjoyed and what I have suffered in it. There I went when my heart was too full of pain or pleasure to bear the eye of another. There have I prayed. There have I sent up thanksgivings. There have I wept bitter tears. A new page in its history will commence to-morrow, Frank. I hope, also, a new and fair page in the history of your mind, that inner, private apartment, on which only your own eye and the eye of Infinite Purity can rest. Begin to-morrow to write on that new page the history of conquered selfishness, of truth and purity, of devotion to duty, of a higher love for others, of obedience to the will of God; then this will be a truly happy New Year.

As I have told you, Frank, beforehand, what your New Year's gift is to be, I will tell Harry, if he pleases, what I have got for him."

"Tell it now, Mother. It is so pleasant here by the fire."

"You are to have a nice new desk, with a key to it, all your own."

"O, that's prime, Mother," said Harry; "and where shall I keep it?"

"In my little writing room, if you like, Harry."

"Yes, Mother; and then I can talk a little now and then to you, I suppose."

"Sometimes, Harry; and I doubt not that Frank will let you come, now and then, to his closet. I don't want this closet to separate you; but, on the contrary, to be the means of making you better friends, because it will help Frank to be a better boy, and so always to set you a good example."

"It is rather hard, Mother, for a boy to set a good example. I don't think I ever did such a thing in my life."

"Mother," said Harry, "you told us that you had been translating a little story from a French book, to read to us some evening. We shall have time enough to-night, for you know you promised to let us sit up till the clock strikes twelve; so we can talk, and read, and tell stories too. There will be time enough for all, before Mr. Old Year goes out and Mr. New Year comes in."

Mrs. Chilton consented. Frank placed her little stand by her, with the German lamp upon it, in the way she liked to have it, and she read as follows:—

THE BIRTHDAY

Near the coast of Northumberland, at a little distance from the land, you can just see rising up a group of little islands, rocks scattered without order, that grow in number at low water; you may count as many as twenty of them, whose sharp, menacing crests seem to defy the returning waves.

Nothing can be more desolate than the appearance of the little Farne Islands; formed of rocks barely covered with a thin vegetation, surrounded by precipices, they seem accessible only to sea birds, who take refuge there in the tempests.

The Island of Longstone is at the head of the group, and serves as a sort of vanguard, and is, perhaps, the most dangerous of all. A gloomy collection of black rocks, full of crevices worn by the action of the winds, the waters, and the tempests, it does not nourish a single plant; not an atom of soil adheres to its surface; it is naked and barren; its steep sides bristle with cockle shells which encrust the rock.

The interior is still more desolate than the exterior; it is a succession of black hillocks cut by narrow ravines into which the sea rushes, roaring and furious, at high tide, detaching from the rocks fragments which it grinds, rounds into pebbles, and deposits pell-mell with the mud and sea weed in some deep crevice, where it again will come to seek them in the storm, roll them over once more in its foam, and drag them off to its profound caverns.

While our feet were wounded by the rocks, above our heads hundreds of sea birds hovered screaming, and among them we discovered the sea-gull by its shrill and harsh scream.

Notwithstanding these horrors, this island is not a desert. At the summit of the rock, there rises a round tower where every evening a light is kindled, so contrived as, at intervals of some seconds, to throw a brilliant light upon the points where the fretted waves rage and boil round a hidden rock, and to light the dangerous channel which separates the island from its sister isles, and to warn the pilot to avoid by every means the perilous labyrinth.

The keeper of the lighthouse did not live alone in this wild place; his wife followed him there; his family increased, and the cradle has rocked again and again.

Grace Darling, the eldest of the seven children, has just reached her twenty-second year, and all the family are rejoicing at the festival, for every anniversary is religiously kept by the little company that animates the solitude of Longstone.

Every one is gone out to seek something by which he may take his part in the festivity, and prepare a surprise for the well-beloved sister. The mother remains at home kneading a nice cake to gratify the appetite of the little marauders.

"Mother, Mother!" cried John, who returned the first; "see what a superb lobster the rising sea has brought up and left in the crevice of a rock, which I call my fish-trap. Might not one say that the sea knew that it was Grace's feast day?"

"I have only some shrimps," said William; "but they are very fine ones, I hope. I took them, with a net at the end of the little creek."

"Imprudent boy!" said their mother; "your father has told you a hundred times not to venture to fish on that side of the island; the rock is too steep, and the water is more than a hundred fathoms deep."

"Yes, but, in a turning, there is a little platform which I have shown to my father, and he has consented to my going there at low water. Then I know the rock, and the sea knows me; neither of them wish to hurt me. You have more reason for scolding Jenny; she is not afraid of any thing; she climbs like a cat all along the crevices to collect sea weed, which she burns in order to enrich the hole which she calls her garden, and to cultivate—what? nothing that one can eat—some good-for-nothing flowers, which grow only in consequence of shelter and great care."

"And you count it for nothing to be able to present to Grace a rose like that?" said Jenny, who just then came in bringing a rose of a dull white, surrounded by vigorous leaves of a dark green. "What a pleasure to have been able to keep it till now, even here, and to see it blossom so exactly at the right time. I do not regret the pains I have taken with it, I assure you."

"And you are right," replied her mother; "for Grace will know well how to appreciate the pains you must have taken to give her such a pleasure; and I, too, approve of the forethought you have discovered, which will make you one day a good housewife. Let your brothers fish and hunt; let it be your care to plant and ornament our solitude with your little smiling, blooming nook of earth."

"But where is Grace?" asked John; "why is she not assisting you as usual, Mother?"

"Because I refused to let her do so. She knows well that this day will be her festival, and I have sent her up stairs to her father, whilst we are here together preparing for her."

"James and the two little ones are missing," said William.

"Only James," replied his mother. "The two little ones are with Grace, who is giving them a lesson in reading. I do not see why James stays away so long; it is nightfall, and his father has always desired him to take care not to be overtaken by a fog far from the house."

"Suppose I go after him," said William.

"There he comes, there he comes!" cried John and Jenny.

The boy came in, in truth, all out of breath.

"I have just succeeded," said he, "in making up the dozen." As he said this, he put upon the table a dozen of wild eggs. "The last came near costing me very dear," said he; "it was laid half way down to the Black Man's; you know, William, the great rock which looks like a giant sitting down; I had climbed, on my knees, and I had only one more step to take, when a great big wave—a coward!—behind struck me, and would have carried me away if I had not clung with all my might to the great Black Man."

"Foolish child," said the mother, "could you not foresee the return of the tide?"

"Not at all, not at all. It came before the hour. There are enormous waves in the channel, and the sea growls as when it is going to be angry."

"That will not prevent us from passing a merry evening," replied William; "come, let us go quickly to work."

He hastened to set the table, and assist his sister in putting on the plates, while his mother broke the eggs, beat up the omelet, and drew out the cake from the oven.

All was ready, and William rang the bell to call the father and Grace to supper, who usually remained in the upper part of the tower of the lighthouse.

Grace loved to contemplate the indented coast of Northumberland, and to see with her naked eyes, of a clear day, the little hamlet where she was born; it was not that she regretted the fertile soil, the verdure, the wood she had seen when she was little. No! the Isle of Longstone, did it not contain in its rocky bosom what was dearest to Grace? Her sympathy extended, however, far beyond. She trembled with joy when she distinguished on board of a passing vessel boys and girls, young people and women. She waved her handkerchief to them, sent to them affectionate words which the wind blew away, but which eased her full heart. She had another more intimate tie to her fellow-beings, and to her native land, and this was the reading some good books, that inexhaustible source of elevated thought and profitable example.

When she at last appeared in the low hall where they waited for her, there was a general hurrah; the question was, who should first get his arms round her neck, who should embrace her, and who should congratulate her on her birthday. She showed herself as much surprised, as much delighted, as the young providers of the festival could desire. She praised the beauty of the lobster, the size of the shrimps, the wild taste of the omelet; but the rose touched her the most tenderly, and Jenny clapped her hands as she said,—

"I was very sure that you would love my poor little flower, which William despised because it was not good to eat."

"He is a little gourmand," said Grace, laughing, "whom I condemn for his punishment to eat my part of the cake."

"To the health of Grace," said the father. "We have just opened for her one of the bottles of old Bourdeaux, which the brave French captain gave us, who came near perishing down below at the end of the great reef of rocks, sixteen years ago."

"And whom you saved at the risk of your life," added his wife.

"I remember it all," said Grace, with a very serious look; "I was very small, yet I well remember that terrible night. I hear now the howling of the waves as they broke against the rocks, and made the lighthouse tremble."

"It was just such a night as this," said the father; "a Friday, the sixth of September. The sun set, just as it set to-night, in a cloud red as blood, which is never a sign of any thing good."

"It is a sign of a great wind," said James; "so much the better; the wild birds will come to the island for shelter."

"A great storm," said John, "always brings fish into my trap; besides, I love the storm."

"Let us play hit-hand," said Jenny. "Come, James, you begin; put your head in my lap, and hold your hand out. There! tell me who struck."

"That is not difficult; it was you."

"O! you looked!"

"No. Now it is your turn."

After this game came blind man's buff. The eldest sister gave herself up to all their wishes. She let them bandage her eyes, and sought fearfully the little fugitives; but notwithstanding her efforts, and the efforts of all to be amused, a cloud hung over the little assembly. Without, a thick fog enveloped the island, and veiled the friendly light.

"If I am not greatly deceived, this will be a very bad night," said the father. "There is, fortunately, no vessel in sight, if it is not, perhaps, the Hull packet, which will have had time, I think, to reach the Bay of Berwick, and which will have the discretion, I trust, to remain there; for the heavens speak in a loud voice this evening; the wind comes from below, and the waves run before it like a flock of frightened sheep."

"I should like to see a flock of sheep," said the little girl of five, whom Grace held in her lap, and whom she was getting to sleep.

"Hush! did I not hear something?" said the mother.

"It is the wind that sings us to sleep in the tower," said the little child.

Grace, who was just going up stairs, stopped and listened. "I only hear the sea which strikes and rages against the rocks," said she.

"Let it beat as it will, it will not wake me," said John. "I am too weary."

Good nights were exchanged, and they all betook themselves to bed; and, in a quarter of an hour after, every one slept, rocked by the storm which roared around the tower, beat against the lighthouse, shook its thick glass, and sought in vain to reach the flame. The tempest increased from hour to hour. It rose in mountainous waves, and broke against the rocks with a tremendous noise.

These sounds were heard in Grace's dreams; she thought she saw men and women struggling with the waves; they called her to their rescue; she held out her hand, and felt herself drawn into the gulf with them. Presently she heard a cry. She sat up in her bed; the day began to dawn; it might be four o'clock in the morning. The wind brought to her ear a cry shriller than the first. This time she was not mistaken; it was a human voice.

Her whole heart was agitated. Quickly as possible she climbed to the steps that led to the outer platform of the lighthouse. Her father was there before her. Clinging to the balustrade, he looked all around; but his eyes were unable to see through the fog and the rain; he saw nothing.

"Grace," said he, "you have good eyes; see if you can discover any thing."

The young girl took the spy glass, but the fog obscured the glasses. She calmly wiped them, and looked again.

"I perceive the top of a mast," said she.

"Where is it?"

"At the head of the long reef. O God, if the fog would only lift." And the young girl raised an earnest prayer to Heaven.

"Why, Father," she called suddenly, "I see something move. There are many of them; they are waiting for us; let us go."

"You do not think, my child," said her father; "stay here; I will go alone."

"Alone to meet those frightful waves, and no one to guide the helm? That would be to go to a certain death. I am stronger than you. Think of no such thing, Father. I shall go with you, and we will save them."

Her father looked in her face, and his eyes filled with tears.

"So be it," he said; "we will die together."

"We will live, and we will save them. Let us to the work."

She hurried on her father. In the twinkling of an eye, the boat, moored in a creek, was unfastened, and launched upon the boiling waves, when a voice cried from the shore,—

"And will you leave me behind? I have a right to run the same risks with you; I wish to take my part." The mother threw herself into the bark, which rose for a moment on the menacing crest of an enormous wave, then disappeared, swallowed up in the furrow left between two mountains of water.

In the mean while, the fog lifted, and a group of shipwrecked people were seen clinging to the sharp points of a ledge of rocks upon which beat the hull of a ship, split in two.

"They come nearer," cried one of them. "O, that terrible wave has carried them farther off."

"Let us thank God for that," said the captain; "it might have dashed them against the reef."

"They will arrive too late," said a poor mother who pressed to her heart an infant already stiff and motionless with cold.

"They are making superhuman efforts," said the captain. "Courage, brave hearts!" And he raised a white handkerchief.

The mother uttered a loud cry. She had just discovered that the child that she was trying to warm was dead.

At this moment, the bark made a desperate effort to land; but a furious wave carried it off for a third time. It whirled round and round, as if taken into one of those bottomless gulfs which the currents form around the rocks, and disappeared.

The group of shipwrecked sufferers, six men and five women, fell upon their knees at this awful moment. Suddenly they perceived the boat nearer to them than ever. It had rounded the reef, and gained a quieter sea. It was coming along the edge of the rock, which on that side sunk precipitately into the sea.

"Bless me," said the captain, "they are women."

"Angels come down from heaven to save us," cried a sailor.

Grace had already seized hold of the poor mother. She had gently taken the dead baby out of her arms, under the pretence of carrying it for her. She led her over the rough parts of the rock into the boat.

There was not a minute to lose; the tide was rising; a delay of a few moments might render a return impossible. The heroic young girl insisted only that she would remain on the reef till the skiff, which could only take half of the company, returned for the remainder.

God rewarded her faith and courage. All those who had been wrecked on the frightful reefs of Longstone were saved, and brought in safety into the small dwelling of the lighthouse.

The remains of the feast, the old wine opened in honor of Grace, helped to reanimate the poor shipwrecked sufferers who owed their lives to the young girl.

"Never was a birthday," as the good mother often said, "so full of terrible and joyful emotions; never was one more blessed."

"That is a right good story, Mother," said Harry. "Was Grace Darling a real person?"

"Yes," said his mother, "and many more beautiful stories are told of her, and all true. She was a noble creature."

"One more story, dear Mother," said the boys. "We have a good deal of time, yet."

"Many years ago," said the mother, "I was making a visit in a family where what I am going to relate to you took place. I wrote it all down, and I will now read it to you from my manuscript book."

A TRUE STORY

One cold, stormy evening in the middle of winter, a family, consisting of four children and their parents, were gathered round a bright, blazing fire. One merry-looking little girl was sitting with a large, beautiful cat in her lap, which she was stroking, while Miss Puss was purring her satisfaction at her happy lot. An older girl was assisting her mother, who was employed at some needlework. The oldest boy was getting his lesson. The youngest was sitting on his father's knee. "How the wind roars!" said little Robert, as a tremendous blast came swelling and moaning over the fields and rushed against their dwelling, which, saving one old elm tree that bent its protecting branches over it, stood all alone, exposed to the shock of the wind against it. "Shan't we blow over, Father?" said the child. "No, dear; we have stood higher winds than this." "Now it dies away," said Helen, as, for a moment, she stopped caressing her favorite. "The storm is taking breath," said Ned; "now you can hear it a great way off; it sounds like a troop of horse galloping up—now it comes nearer and nearer. Hurrah! there it comes again! hurrah! Hear the poor old elm creak and groan, and hear the icicles rattling down. I hope none of the branches will break, but I am afraid the ice is too heavy for them." "Think of poor old Fanny to-night," said Julia, the elder girl, "in her little cottage, and the walls so thin. Mother, what will she do?" "Her house is so small that the wind seems to pass her by," said the mother, "and, when it is so cold as it is to-night, the poor soul goes to bed, and lies there till it is warmer. Many a time, I have found her in bed in the morning, and given her some breakfast, and advised her to lie there till she could get up with comfort." "It is so still now," said Robert, "that I can hear the flakes of snow on the window panes." "And so do I," said little Helen, "and the wind seems to say, Hush! hush!" "I should not think you could hear any thing while Puss is purring so loud in your ears," replied Ned. "Do put her out of the room; I would rather hear the loudest wind that ever blew than hear a cat purr, purr, purr so forever; it makes my head spin to hear it; hush, Puss! stop purring." Puss purred on all the same, for Ned's words were followed by no hostile act towards her. No one, much less Helen's pet, was ever treated inhospitably at Mr. Nelson's fireside.

Now there was a short silence in the happy group, and nothing was heard but the fitful wind without, the crackling of the fire, and the contented sound of the purring cat within. Mrs. Nelson was the first to speak. "Is it not time," said she, "for John to return from the village? I cannot help expecting a letter from James. If,"—and the color left her cheeks,—"if he was alive and well, I am sure he must have written, and we must have a letter by Captain S." "I hear John coming up the avenue now." In a moment Ned was gone to see what packages were brought from the office, and in another he was back again with a parcel in his hand. "Here, Father," said he, "here are the newspapers, and here, Mother, is a big letter from uncle John for you."

His mother opened her brother's letter. "A letter from Jemmy," said she, with a voice trembling with joy. "A letter from Jemmy," said all the children together, and in a moment each one was silent, in order to listen to its contents.

"Dear Mother: Here we are all safe and sound; but when you get this, you will, I know, thank God you have yet a son Jemmy. I have kept a sea journal which you and father can see when I get home; so I shall say nothing more about our voyage, except that I got along very well, considering I was a green hand, and that I made friends with the mates and all the sailors. O, they were so kind to me! and lucky it was for me that they did love me so well, as you'll see presently. Well, to my story. I hate to come to it, for it makes me feel so badly; but don't be frightened, Mother; here I am on shore, as lively as a cricket, and could make as much noise in your house now as I ever did. Well, dear Mother, all, as I said, went well with me, till one night, when we were on the Grand Bank; it was a rain storm, and the captain sent me up to the topmast to reef a sail; some one had been up, in the course of the day, and dropped some grease, and I think my foot slipped; I was confused, the rain beat in my face, I could not see any thing, and I fell. I must have been stunned, for I am sure some time must have passed before I found myself overboard, struggling to keep myself above water. In a moment, I saw my whole danger. I knew that the ship must have gone on some distance, and that it was useless to try to swim after her. I did not think the sailors would know I had fallen overboard, for some time, and I knew that, in such a dark, stormy night, it was almost impossible for them to do any thing to save me. You know, dear Mother, I am an excellent swimmer; but I immediately thought that my only chance was to save my strength as much as possible; so I turned over on my back and floated, and determined to keep myself as quiet as I could, so as not to exhaust myself before the boat could come for me, which was what I hoped for, though I knew there was small chance of it, on such a night. In a few moments I saw indistinctly one of those great birds that follow after vessels, hovering over me, and I felt his horrid wings brushing over my face. I used one of my arms to drive him away, while, with the other, I kept myself on the top of the water; the waves rolled high, and, as they broke over me, repeatedly filled my mouth with the bitter water, so that I could not scream to let any one know where I was. Presently more birds, smaller however, fluttered their frightful wings over me; but the large one, whose wings I am sure extended as far as I could stretch my arms, was the worst; he kept hovering over me; O, I can see the frightful creature now! Well, Mother, don't be scared, for here I am as well as ever. I found my strength began to fail me. I could not see the ship. The cold was terrible. The horrid birds were hovering, and the waves were rolling over me. I thought of you and father, my brothers and sisters, my dear home; and I felt as if I could not bear my sufferings any longer, and that I had better give up. I was about turning myself over and letting myself go, when I saw a black thing at a distance which I took for a porpoise. While I was looking to see what it was, I heard the words, 'Jemmy! Jemmy!' and I called out, 'Here I am!' This was the first sound I had been able to make from the time I had fallen over, for if I opened my mouth it filled with water. They soon had me in the boat, and, soon after, I was in the ship. Every thing was done for me, that love and kindness could do. I could not have held out much longer. It was three quarters of an hour that I had been in the water. They told me afterwards that when they found I had fallen overboard, they put the ship about; but as they heard no sound from me, and knew not whereabouts I had fallen, the captain said it was useless to do any thing to save me. The steward and cook and one of the men were getting out the boat, but it had a bad leak in it, and the captain advised them not to go. They would not listen to him; they said they would not give me up; and they lowered the boat. One of the men baled all the time, and as he had nothing else to stop the leak with, he put his foot in the place, and he kept the boat above water. By the merest chance they steered directly for the spot where I was. So you see, Mother, it was their love and their courage that saved my life."

"Now, dear Mother, you will not feel anxious about me any more, for I think you may be sure that nothing worse will happen to me than has happened already on this voyage. I hope to be with you in a month after you got this, and I don't think I shall want to go to sea again for one while. My love to father and the boys, and to Julia, and Helen, and the cat, and all inquiring friends. Glad enough I shall be to be with you all again. I never knew before, dear Mother, how much I loved you all. Your affectionate son, Jemmy."

"P.S. After my fall I could not stand for a fortnight, but they all took the kindest care of me, and I am now as well as possible."

It were vain to attempt to describe what passed in the hearts of these parents at hearing of the safety of their son after such a peril. The letter was read over and over again, and each one expressed his happiness in his own way; little Helen wondered he should have thought of Puss, but said it was just like Jemmy. "I would not believe such a story if I had it from any other but James himself," said his father. "Nothing, so uncommon as to save a person that falls overboard in such a way; and at night I never knew of it, and I have been many years at sea. Nothing but James's presence of mind and courage saved his life; he did the only thing that would have been of any avail; had he attempted to swim after the ship, he would have been lost. It seems now as if the story could not be true. His presence of mind, and his courage, and his knowledge of swimming would, however, have been of little use to him, if the love of the sailors for him had not been stronger than the love of their own lives, which they put in the greatest peril to save this poor boy who, a few weeks before, was an utter stranger to them. How noble! how beautiful! The glory of the wise and so-called great of this world fades away as we look at this simple act of self-devoted love. In the hearts of each of these men we see the angel that God has placed within us all, ever declaring, if we would listen, that love is greater than life, that there is no death to the soul."

The children, not long after, retired to bed; the thought of dear brother Jemmy made them insensible to the storm; all was sunshine and peace in their young hearts. The parents sat up many hours of that stormy night talking over and over again the story of their boy's imminent danger and of his miraculous escape.

The hoarse breathings of the wild storm, its alternate deep, far-off moaning and shrill piping, through every loophole and crevice in the house, sounded to these heaven-attuned souls like solemn music, and they joined in sweet accord in silent, grateful prayer to the Infinite Spirit.

Frank and Harry, with their mother, were now silent for a few moments. Soon, slowly and solemnly, the bell struck one, two, three, four, five, six, and so on to twelve, and the first moment of the new year began to be. They kissed each other, said "Happy New Year," and were soon fast asleep in bed.